Anna Wilson lives in Northamptonshire with her husband, David, and her children, Lucy and Thomas. She has two black cats called Ink and Jet and a Labrador to match called Kenna. She has written two picture books and plans many more books in the

Nina
Fairy Ballerina
series.

Nicola Slater lives in the north of England with Dave the cat. Her work can be seen on books and tablecloths around the globe.

D0316283

Look out for the other books in the

Nina Fairy Ballerina series

New Girl

Daisy Shoes

Best Friends

Show Time

Flying Colours

Coming soon

Party Magic

Dream Treat

Compiled by Anna Wilson

Princess Stories

Fairy Stories

Nina
Fairy Ballerina

Double Trouble

Anna Wilson

Illustrated by Nicola Slater

MACMILLAN CHILDREN'S BOOKS

First published 2006 by Macmillan Children's Books
a division of Macmillan Publishers Limited
20 New Wharf Road, London N1 9RR
Basingstoke and Oxford
www.panmacmillan.com

Associated companies throughout the world

ISBN-13: 978-0-330-44620-4
ISBN-10: 0-330-44620-7

Text copyright © Anna Wilson 2006
Illustrations copyright © Nicola Slater 2006

1 3 5 7 9 8 6 4 2

A CIP catalogue record for this book is available from
the British Library.

Typeset by Nigel Hazle
Printed and bound in Great Britain by Mackays of Chatham plc, Kent

For David, for everything

Chapter One

"Isn't it fantastic to be back?" Bella shouted, zooming through the corridors of the Royal Academy of Fairy Ballet.

"Oh yes! The Second Year's going to be great," Nina replied, fluttering after her excitedly.

"I really want to be a mentor," she added.

"No way — not me!" Peri exclaimed. "I just want to have fun with you guys. I don't want any boring duties, thanks very much."

Bella was the first of the three to fly at full pelt into the Grand Hall, where Madame Dupré and the other teachers were already sitting on their golden chairs on the stage. The headmistress smiled as her favourite fairy ballerinas fluttered in to take their places next to the other Second Years, who were buzzing with excitement, their wings whirring.

It really *does* feel great to be back, Nina thought happily. She caught sight of Nyssa Bean, one of her classmates, and they grinned at each other and waved.

The rest of the fairy ballerinas filed in and waited for Miss Meadowsweet, the

Academy secretary, to bring in the new
First Years. They soon arrived, nervously
fluttering behind the secretary, not
daring to look up at the fairies filling
the hall.

"Don't be shy, dears," Madame
Dupré called out kindly. "Come to the
front. You will soon feel at home."

The new fairies curtseyed clumsily.
Then Madame Dupré waved her wand
to attract the attention of all her pupils.
The hall filled with silver stardust, which
shimmered as it fell down on the fairy
ballerinas. They immediately stood tall,
arms held in front of their bodies in a
gentle oval shape, feet in first position –
the picture of perfection.

"Now, Second Years," said Madame
Dupré, looking down at Nina's row, "I
am sure you remember how you were
welcomed to the Academy last year."
The Second Years nodded seriously,
feeling very important. "Now it is your

turn to be helpful and kind to the new First Years," the headmistress continued.

"Helpful and kind?" Peri hissed to Nina. "That's not how I remember *your* mentor!"

Nina grimaced at the memory of how nasty Angelica Nightshade had been.

"So, if we are *all* listening, fairies . . ." the headmistress was saying, glaring at Nina and Peri, "let's see the list of this

year's mentors and who they will be looking after."

Madame Dupré waved her wand. A huge whiteboard appeared behind the row of teachers. She tapped the board with her wand and a stream of silver ink flowed and began to write. The fairy ballerinas chattered among themselves, trying to guess who would be on the list.

Nina didn't join in the gossiping though. The colour in her face slowly drained away until she looked as white as the board itself. She was staring at it in utter disbelief.

"Hey, what's the matter, Nina?" Peri asked, putting a hand on her friend's shoulder. "You look awful."

Nina pointed a shaky finger at the board and whispered, "It can't be true."

Nina's name was there in silver ink.

"Hey, you're a mentor. That's fab!" Bella cried. But then she looked at the name next to Nina's.

"Holly *Nightshade*," Peri read out in dismay.

"Exactly," said Nina. "Angelica's little sister!"

Nina Dewdrop & Holly Nightshade

Chapter Two

Madame Dupré asked the First Years to remain behind after assembly so that she could introduce them to their mentors. The rest of the fairy ballerinas took off down the corridor to the ballet studios, but Nina and her friends were still in a huddle. Peri and Bella didn't want to leave Nina feeling so upset.

"I can't believe I'm looking after a Nightshade!" Nina complained. "After everything Angelica did last year . . . I just can't face it!"

"Don't worry, Nina," Bella said reassuringly. "Look, I could take your place and be Holly's mentor instead. Let's just have a chat with Madame and see—"

"No," Nina said, shaking her head. She wiped away a stray tear and took a deep breath. "Madame must know what she's doing. Anyway," she added bravely, "Holly can't possibly be as bad as her older sister – can she?"

Holly hovered, waiting for Nina to show her around the Academy. Nina looked at the tiny blonde First Year.

She looks too

small to be much trouble, Nina thought.
She even looks quite sweet in that pink
tutu. And what a cute pink rose she's got
in her hair. Angelica might have been
horrid to me, but I am going to make
sure that her sister will have nothing to
complain about.

Nina decided to take Holly to her
room first.

"You must be a bit nervous," she said
to Holly kindly. "I was lucky: my mum
and little sister came with me on my first
day. We didn't meet our mentors till
later. But don't worry, you'll soon find
your way around and make friends. Do
you know who your room-mate is?"

"I'm not sharing with anyone," said
Holly rather scornfully. "I do enough of
that at home. I don't like sharing."

Nina sighed quietly. Holly already
sounded exactly like her older sister.

"Well, we all share here at the
Academy," Nina explained patiently. "I

have two room-mates actually: Peri and—"

"Bella Glove. Yeah, I know," Holly interrupted rudely. "Angelica's already told me. But then, you're a scholarship fairy, aren't you, so you probably can't afford to have your own room. And your friend Peri's not exactly rolling in money either, is she?" Holly added, sneering.

"It's got nothing to do with money," Nina said sharply. She was about to add that Bella came from a very wealthy background, but she didn't get a chance.

"We've got *pots and pots* of fairy gold in our family," Holly boasted, "so Mummy's arranged for me to have my own room. It's on Charlock corridor," she added, looking up slyly at Nina.

Oh no! Nina groaned to herself. We're neighbours! This gets worse and worse.

"So . . . Holly's a nice name," Nina

said, trying in desperation to make
conversation.

"It's Hollyhock, actually," Holly said,
smoothing down her long blonde hair
that was every bit as shiny and
glamorous as her older sister's. "But that's
too tricky for most common or garden
fairies to cope with."

"Right," Nina said, feeling
increasingly irritated with the miniature
madam's behaviour. She made yet
another attempt at friendly chit-chat:
"Well, it's nice for you to have your
sister at the Academy, isn't it?"

Holly shrugged her wings and said,
"Whatever."

"I'm sure she'll help you settle in,"
Nina said, still trying to be kind.

"I thought that was *your* job," Holly
snapped.

Maybe Angelica told Holly to stay
out of her way. I wouldn't put it past
her, Nina thought.

She beckoned to Holly to follow, but the tiny fairy elbowed past her mentor and whizzed off ahead, wings whirring, leaving a trail of pink glitter in her wake.

"I don't need *you* to show me the way!" she called over her shoulder. "Angelica's already told me where to find my room."

"It's a pity *she's* not your mentor then," Nina muttered under her breath as she flew reluctantly after the First Year.

♦ Chapter Three ♦

Nina spotted Holly flying into room six on Charlock corridor. She caught up with the little fairy at last.

"You're next door to me!" she said,

trying to disguise the dismay in her voice. "I'm in room five. Bella, Peri and I have the same room as last year because we've got a special triple bunk bed . . ." She tailed off.

Holly wasn't listening. She was too busy scrabbling about, trying to push the spare bed back into the window seat. All the rooms had a spare bed so that if a guest came they would have somewhere to stay.

"What are you doing?" Nina asked, puzzled. "I thought you said you weren't sharing your room with anyone?"

"Oh, er, the spare bed was sticking out," Holly said carelessly. "Typical! Angelica said the staff were slapdash," the haughty fairy added, tossing her hair over her shoulders.

Nina took a deep breath and, ignoring Holly's last comment, she smiled sweetly and said, "Let's get unpacked, shall we? I'll help you put

your clothes away. Should we check
you have everything you need, first of
all? Gosh, you do have a lot of stuff,"
Nina added, frowning, as she caught
sight of a mountain of suitcases and a
very expensive-looking pink ballet
bag.

"Yeah, don't I?" Holly replied
smugly. "Mummy
ordered everything
from Marks &
Sparklers – it's *the*
place for ballet
clothes this
year." She looked
Nina up and down
and pulled a face.
"Although by the looks
of it, *you've* never
been there."

Nina gritted her teeth.
"Tell you what, you
take your time

unpacking. I've got a few of my own
things to sort out. If you need me you
can find me next door."

Holly ignored her, as she was already
engrossed in pulling bundles of soft,
shimmering silk tights from a silver bag
with M & S embossed on the side.

Little madam! Nina thought, fuming.
She left the room, her wings crackling in
indignation. Wait till I tell the others
about her.

She fluttered next door, where she
found Peri and Bella sitting cosily on
the bottom bunk, clapping and laughing
loudly at – Holly! The tiny First Year
was already dressed in her regulation
turquoise leotard and crossover
cardigan and was giving a convincing
demonstration of her ballet skills. How
in all fairyland did she slip past me
so fast? Nina wondered. *And* she's
changed the flower in her hair to a
tulip!

Holly was having a wonderful time showing off.

"And this is how my teacher does a grand plié in fifth position," she was saying. She tucked her left foot neatly behind her right and gently bent her knees until her thighs were parallel with

the floor. Her back was ramrod straight;
she didn't wobble at all.

"Wow!" Bella cried enthusiastically.
"Looks like you've got some competition,
Nina," she added, noticing her friend for
the first time.

Nina tried to fix what she hoped was
a cheery grin on to her face. "Yes, that's
very impressive, Holly," she said.

"Yeah, well, I would have got a
scholarship too, you know," the little
fairy replied, sighing dramatically, "but I
couldn't be bothered to apply."

"You don't need one anyway," Nina
retorted. "You told me that you have
'pots of fairy gold'."

"No, I didn't!" Holly protested.

"Yes, you did—"

"Hey, hey – guys!" Bella interrupted
anxiously. "Don't argue."

Nina shrugged. "What are you doing
in here anyway, Holly?"

"Holly got lost," Peri explained. "We

found her wandering about in the
corridor."

"Got lost?"
Nina was
puzzled. "But
I left you in
your room five
seconds ago.
And it's only
next door. How
can you have had
time to get
changed *and*
get lost?"

Chapter Four

Holly didn't bother answering Nina, as just then the bluebell rang for the first class of the term. Nina had been told to take Holly to meet her teacher, but once again the new girl was too quick for her. She shot down the corridor in a cloud of light blue sparkles before Nina could say "fairy dust".

"Lead on, Holly," Nina muttered wearily, waving goodbye to her friends.

"This way, slow-wings!" Holly jeered over her shoulder. "I bet you didn't know this short cut to class!"

Nina was puzzled. Holly seemed to be heading towards the toilets.

I'm sure there's no short cut through there, Nina thought.

But she followed the trail of blue sparkles anyway, as it was not easy to argue in mid-flight. Suddenly Holly curtseyed cheekily to Nina and turned a corner unexpectedly.

"Holly? Where are you?" Nina shouted angrily. The little imp had vanished so quickly that Nina wasn't sure whether she really *had* gone into the toilets.

I'd better check there first, Nina thought. She went in and called out:

"Are you OK, Holly? You'd better hurry up."

No answer.

Nina checked the cubicles – they were all empty.

"She's tricked me!" Nina shouted. "This is a typical Nightshade nightmare. What is it with that family? I suppose I'll have to go to the First-Years' studio and explain that Holly flew away from me. How embarrassing."

Nina arrived at the studio flushed and angry. The class had already started. The First-Years' teacher was Miss Marram. She was a young, graceful fairy, dressed from top to toe in green. Her tutu was soft and feathery, and her hair was tied in a little tuft on top of her head. She was demonstrating how a ballerina turns out her feet so that her legs are at right angles to her hips.

Nina stopped in the doorway to watch. She suddenly felt a bit sad.

The First Year had been such fun –
everything had been so new and exciting.
She was beginning to realize that being a
mentor wasn't all she had hoped it would
be, and she felt rather out of her depth.

She was abruptly jolted out of her
daydreaming at the sight of a
familiar mane of blonde hair
swishing back and forth.

"Holly!" she called
out. She noticed that
Holly was
wearing the
pink rose in her hair
again. What a vain
little madam, Nina said to
herself, changing her
outfits all the time . . .

Miss Marram stopped
her demonstration and
frowned.

"I know this is the first day
back, but I do object to having

my class interrupted," she said firmly. "What is the matter?"

"Please, Miss Marram, I'm Nina Dewdrop and—" Nina began.

"I know that, dear," Miss Marram cut in. "You were supposed to bring Holly to class, but she tells me that you forgot and that she had to find her own way here."

Nina breathed in sharply and was about to protest, but Holly didn't give her time. Putting on her best sad-puppy-dog face, the sly fairy wheedled, "It wasn't very nice of you, Nina. I am only a little First Year, after all."

Miss Marram folded her slim arms across her chest and looked hard at Nina. "I would have expected better of our scholarship fairy. Please make sure you are here to pick Holly up at the end of class."

Nina was speechless – which was just as well, as she could see she wasn't going to be given a chance to tell her side of the story. She curtseyed and mumbled, "Yes, Miss Marram." Then she flew slowly out of the studio, her wings dragging and tears pricking in her eyes.

"Being a mentor to that trickster is definitely not going to be a piece of fairy cake," she thought miserably.

Chapter Five

The mysterious muddle with Holly had made Nina late for her own class. Luckily she was to be taught by Miss Tremula again this term. Fairy ballerinas did not usually keep the same teacher two years running. However, Miss Tremula was going to be retiring after her one hundredth birthday, and she had especially requested that she keep Nina's class until then, as she was so fond of them.

"Nina, dear! Whatever is the matter? Your wings are all a-flutter. Are you

unwell?" Miss Tremula
asked, concerned
for her star
pupil.

Nina put on a
brave smile.
"No, miss,"
she replied.
"There was just a
bit of a mix-up with the
fairy I'm mentoring. I'm
so sorry I'm late," she
added, curtseying.

"It's all right, dear,"
Miss Tremula said
kindly. "I know it's
not like you. Come and
join us. I was just telling
the class what will be
expected of you now
that you are in your Second Year."

Nina smiled properly this time. She
took her place at the barre in between

Bella and Peri, feeling happily at home.

"As you know," Miss Tremula was saying, "I will be leaving you all at some point next term—"

The fairy ballerinas started crying out, "Don't go, Miss T!"

Miss Tremula laughed, holding up her walking stick, which doubled as a wand. "A fairy can't go on teaching forever, my dears! And besides, I am looking forward to my retirement. I'm going to fly around fairyland and visit the places I've always dreamed of exploring . . ." Miss Tremula gazed wistfully out of the window as if mentally planning her route. Then she shook her wings out briskly and snapped back to the present. "In the meantime," she said in her normal, efficient voice, "I am determined that you will impress your new teacher, so this term we will be working hard to prepare you for pointe work."

"What's that?" asked Hazel Leafbud, one of Nina's friends.

"Can anyone explain to Hazel what pointe work is?" Miss Tremula asked the class. Nina put up her hand. "Yes, Nina?"

"It's when a ballerina dances on the tips of her toes in special pointe shoes," Nina replied eagerly.

"That's right. A pointe shoe is certainly very special," Miss Tremula agreed. "The shoes are very hard at the tip, which makes them extremely difficult to dance in. I've brought a pair for you to see," she added, handing a pair of pale pink ballet shoes to Bella. "Pass them round, dear," the teacher commanded.

"Wow, they're weird!" Bella cried as she took the shoes. "They're so stiff! What are they made of?"

"The main part of the shoe is just like the soft shoes that you are all wearing

now," Miss Tremula explained, "but the tip is made from layers and layers of satin, paper and a hard canvas called burlap, all of which are tightly glued together."

"I tried a pair once – they're agony to dance in!" Peri said, pulling a face.

Miss Tremula smiled. "Don't worry, Peri dear. By the time I've finished with you, you'll be able to dance as gracefully in pointe shoes as if you were floating on a summer breeze!"

Nina sighed as she took the beautiful shoes from Peri. For a moment she

thought she could hear the shoes
whispering to her:

If you want to dance in us
You must work hard — not make a fuss.
You will feel sore sometimes, it's true:
We are not the softest shoe.
But if your feet are good and strong
It really won't be very long
Before you're floating through the air —
Dancing on pointe without a care!

"I thought my daisy shoes were special,"
she murmured, "but these are magical."
She imagined herself wearing them on
stage in front of a distinguished audience.
She would perform a *pas ballonné*: she
would skip along on the tips of her toes,
stretching her left leg out to the side and
then pointing it down into her right leg.
She would hold her arms gracefully out
to the side of her body, her neck long,
she would—

"Nina, did you hear what I said, dear?" Miss Tremula was saying.

Nina jumped. "Oh, sorry, miss," she said, blushing. "I was thinking about dancing on pointe . . ."

Miss Tremula laughed. "I'm afraid it takes more than thinking about it to be able dance in *those* shoes," she said. "So let's get to work, fairies."

Nina beamed, all thoughts of the troublesome Holly forgotten, and was soon lost in what she loved doing best – ballet.

Chapter Six

ina, Peri and Bella zoomed off to get Holly after class.

"That barre work was so hard!" Peri said, running her hands wearily through her spiky red hair. "All those relevés on to demi-pointe! Drama classes were a lot easier on the feet . . . . I'm glad we're allowed to fly to and from lessons — my legs are killing me!"

"I know," Bella agreed. "But it'll be worth it in the end."

"Yes," said Nina. "Remember what Miss Tremula said: if we learn to rise up on to our toes correctly in soft shoes, it will be easier for us when we move into pointe shoes. And I can't wait to try them. They're so beautiful. Imagine performing in them . . ." she added wistfully.

"Miss T kept saying, 'Keep a vertical line through the centre of your feet,'" Bella complained. "I didn't get that at all! How do you keep a line through your feet, for fairyland's sake?"

"Oh, that's easy," Nina explained enthusiastically. "She just means you have to keep your whole body up really straight — it's so that you don't go over on your feet and hurt your ankle or anything. I read about it in a book by

Darling Bushel — you know, the fairy
who used to be headmistress here."

Nina was so busy trying to
demonstrate this while flying that she
didn't look where she was going and flew
right into Holly, who was lurking around
the corner.

"Ouch! Watch it!" Holly shouted,
holding on to her right arm and
making a big fuss.
"You've really hurt my
arm!"

"I'm . . . I'm
sorry," Nina
stammered.
"Here, let
me take a
look."

"Get off me!"
Holly yelled.
"You've done
enough damage
already."

"Hey, calm down," Bella said. "You're overreacting — it was an accident."

"Yeah," Peri agreed. "Nina didn't mean to hurt you."

"And what are you doing hiding in the corridor anyway, Holly?" Nina asked. "I was just coming to get you."

"Yeah, well, don't bother, scholarship slug," Holly snapped rudely. "I'm going to my room for a lie-down. My arm *really* hurts." And she took off towards Charlock corridor in a shower of pink glitter, muttering viciously under her breath.

Nina shook her wings out irritably. "She's even more of a nightmare than her big sister," she muttered.

Peri nodded. "Weird. She seemed so cute earlier. Never mind, let's go to lunch."

Linking arms, the three fairies made their way to the Refectory.

"I've missed school meals," Peri said, sniffing at the delicious aromas in the air. "Mmm — get a load of that! Basil is such a star cook."

Nina cheered up; Peri was a real foodie, and her enthusiasm always made Nina smile. However, her smile soon faded when she saw who was in the Refectory.

"Holly!" Nina cried. "What in the name of enchantment . . . ? You said you were going back to your room."

The impudent imp was sitting at a long table, giggling with her new fairy friends. She looked puzzled when Nina shouted at her, but quickly put on a cheeky grin and waved.

"Hiya! I . . . er . . . I was hungry," Holly said. "Why don't you come and join us." Holly turned to the other First Years. "Guys, this is Nina, my mentor."

"They know that; they saw me in class earlier," Nina said grumpily.

Bella nudged her with her elbow. "Come on, Nina, be nice. Holly obviously wants to make up for shouting at you."

Nina shrugged her wings. "S'pose so," she muttered. Then she noticed Holly's hair again. "Why do you keep changing that flower in your hair, Holly? You were wearing a rose just now," she said suspiciously.

"Er . . . got to keep up with the fashions!" Holly replied quickly. "Not like you, Miss Nina Dulldrop." She giggled, then made a big show of rubbing her left arm and grimacing. "You know, I think I'll go back to my room after all. My arm really hurts."

Nina frowned. "I didn't run into you that hard and, anyway, it was your *right* arm I knocked, wasn't it?"

Holly leaped up as if she'd been stung by a bee. She knocked over acorn cups and plates of food in her haste and cried,

"You don't even care that I'm hurt!
Some mentor you are, Nina Dewdrop."
    And with that, the First-Year fairy
flew off in a huff.

Chapter Seven

Miss Tremula had not been joking when she'd said she wanted her class to work hard. That afternoon the fairies did the same exercises again and again, practising the relevés on to demi-pointe until their legs were stinging.

"I think we've done enough relevés for now," Miss Tremula said at last. The class sighed in relief at this welcome news. "But we're not stopping there," Miss Tremula continued. "I want to see a demi-plié now."

Easy-peasy! Nina thought happily. We learned them in our first term.

"Now, you've all done demi-pliés before," the fairy teacher said, echoing Nina's thoughts, "but this time we are going to do something a little harder. I want you to start in fifth position, like this."

Miss Tremula turned out her right foot and tucked her left foot elegantly behind it. The toe of her left foot was just touching the heel of her right. She bent her knees slowly and lowered herself into a graceful demi-plié. Then all at once, she sprang up on to demi-pointe in second position, her hips beautifully turned out. As she repeated the movement she looked like a little pair of scissors opening and closing.

"I'm sure you can all manage that, dears," she said encouragingly. "Mrs Wisteria, will you play for us, please?" she called out to the pianist.

Mrs Wisteria began a gentle piece from the ballet *Giselle*, and the fairy ballerinas slowly copied the exercise. Gradually the music sped up, forcing the

ballerinas to jump quicker and quicker to keep to the beat.

Peri couldn't manage and fell over, gasping for breath.

Miss Tremula motioned to Mrs Wisteria to stop playing and asked Peri if she was hurt.

"No, no, miss," Peri puffed. "But my legs feel all wobbly like frogspawn!"

Miss Tremula laughed. "Well, we can't have that – my ballerinas are supposed to feel like thistledown, not frogspawn." She picked up the beautiful pointe shoes again and waved them at the class. "You don't see many tadpoles wearing shoes like these!" she joked.

The class was interrupted by a knock on the door. Miss Tremula sighed and put the shoes down on top of the piano. "Come in!" she called irritably.

It was Holly. She was fiddling with the tulip in her hair, trying her best to look lost and confused again.

Nina groaned quietly. What now? she thought.

"Please, miss," said Holly sweetly, "I think Nina's got my ballet bag. Can I come in?"

Nina protested: "How can I have it? You must have left it in your room!"

"Nina," said Miss Tremula gently. "You are Holly's mentor. It is your duty to help her. Come in, Holly, and check the pegs."

Holly whizzed over to the clothes rack next to the piano and made a big performance of riffling through the bags. She threw stray leotards and cardigans over her shoulder in her search, sending blue sparks flying on to the piano.

"Here it is!" she cried, triumphantly brandishing a blue satin bag.

Nina was outraged. "I've no idea how that got there!" she shouted. "Anyway, isn't your bag pink? I saw it in your room . . ."

But Holly just pirouetted cheekily out of the room, calling, "Thank you!" and disappeared.

Nina was sure she caught a glimpse of someone lurking in the corridor, as if they were trying to stay out of sight.

Was that Angelica? Nina wondered. I bet she put Holly up to that little trick.

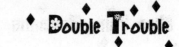

She made for the door, but Miss Tremula called her back.

"Nina! You'd better take more care of Holly's things in future. I won't have class disrupted again." Nina tried to protest, but Miss Tremula held up her

walking stick and stopped her: "Enough!
We must press on. Arms next, fairies."

Nina tried to forget about Holly.

"These advanced arm positions are
known as 'port de bras'," the teacher
explained. "Your arms must look light
and delicate."

First of all the fairies had to learn
how to place their hands so that they
always looked natural and relaxed.

"Fingers must be softly grouped
together," Miss Tremula continued. "I
don't want to see tight, angry fists,
fairies! That's lovely, Nina dear. Now,
watch as I open my hand gently . . . this
is an 'allongé'."

The tiny teacher held her hand with
the palm facing downwards and let her
fingers unfurl softly like the petals of a
bud opening in spring.

"And this position is a 'nuance'," the
teacher went on. "It is a development of

the basic hand position. When you dance
your hands speak for you, so that the
audience knows what you are trying to
say."

"Oh! It's like mime!" Peri cried, her
green eyes sparkling. "I learned about
that this summer, Miss Tremula, when I
did a theatre workshop."

"Really? That's interesting, Periwinkle.
It is like mime, yes. A ballet dancer never
talks while dancing, so her body speaks
for her."

"I think I'm better at talking out
loud, miss," Peri said seriously.

Miss Tremula laughed. "I can't
disagree with you there, dear!" she said.

The fairies went over and over the
new exercises until their wings were
drooping with tiredness.

"I think we should call it a day now,
fairies," Miss Tremula said. "You are
worn out. Collect your bags."

The teacher helped tidy away the

clothes Holly had strewn around the piano earlier.

"Where *did* I put my pointe shoes?" Miss Tremula wondered when she'd finished. "They were here on the piano. Have we put them in one of the bags by mistake?"

Everyone checked, but to no avail.

Miss Tremula started panicking, fluttering around the studio searching high and low. It soon became apparent that the shoes had vanished into thin air.

"Those shoes were given to me years ago by Darling Bushel before she retired as headmistress!" the poor teacher cried. "They are *extremely* precious. If one of you is playing a trick on me and hiding them, there will be dire consequences, fairies!"

And with that warning, Miss Tremula swept out of the classroom in distress.

Chapter Eight ◆

That night, Nina and her friends pulled on their pyjamas and snuggled into their beds in silence; they were exhausted. Bella even forgot to remove her silver hairclips, she was so tired.

Knock, knock!

Miss Marram was at the door, doing lights-out duty.

She looked in and saw that the three friends were already in bed. Waving her wand, she sang the bedtime rhyme:

Golden slumbers, kiss your eyes.
Put out your lights now, fireflies!
Sleep little fairies, have sweet dreams
And rise like happy, bright sunbeams.

A shower of golden stars streamed out from her wand, and the fireflies in the room obediently extinguished their lights.

Peri and Bella just managed a sleepy "Goodnight" before falling asleep.

But although Nina was just as tired as her friends, she couldn't get to sleep immediately: she was upset about what had happened in class. She pulled her pretty patchwork quilt tightly around her and tried in vain to think happy thoughts.

What has happened to those pointe shoes? she wondered. I do hope Miss T finds them. They were so magical.

She started imagining again what it would be like to dance in shoes like that.

She pictured herself at the Royal Fairy
Opera House in Clover Garden,
performing before Queen Camellia and
Princess Coriander . . . and she started to
drift off . . .

Knock, knock!

"Who's there?" Nina cried. She had
been dreaming, but now she was wide
awake and sitting bolt upright in bed.

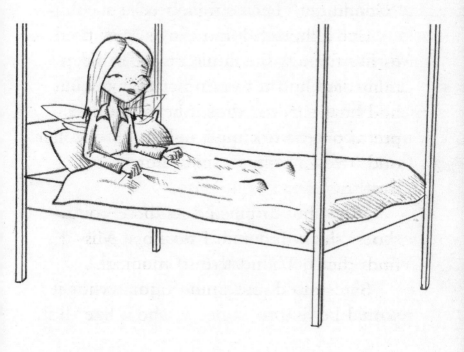

The door opened, and by the dim glow of the fireflies in the corridor Nina could see an angry Miss Marram.

"Nina, I think you've got some explaining to do," whispered the teacher sternly. "Come out here so we don't wake your room-mates."

"What? What is it?" Nina said, feeling panicky. She hopped out of bed and fluttered into the corridor, pulling the door to behind her. Then she noticed a sneaky-looking Holly standing next to Miss Marram. She was still wearing her ballet clothes and had a rose in her hair again.

"Holly tells me that you told her to meet you here to find a hiding place for these!" Miss Marram gestured towards something she was holding.

Nina's jaw dropped in surprise and horror. "Miss Tremula's pointe shoes! Where did you find them?" she cried.

"As if you didn't know!" the teacher retorted.

"Holly must have taken them from the studio," Nina stuttered.

"You're going to have to do better than that, young fairy," Miss Marram said. "You're to come and explain yourself to Madame Dupré first thing in the morning. You've given Miss Tremula a dreadful fright, Nina. And at her age too. It's disgraceful. Now, both of you are to go back to bed at once."

Nina was so baffled she couldn't think of anything to say in her defence. In any case, Miss Marram didn't give her a chance. She waved her wand furiously and vanished.

Nina leaned in close to Holly and hissed, "I don't know what you're up to, Hollyhock Nightshade, but this is one little trick too far."

Chapter Nine

The next day, Peri and Bella were very upset to hear what had happened.

"Don't worry, Nina, we know you didn't take the shoes," said Bella.

"Yeah," Peri agreed. "You'd be dancing off into the sunset with Magnolia Valentine by now!"

"It's not funny, Peri," Nina cried. "I'm sure Angelica's behind all this. In fact, I saw someone hiding in the corridor when Holly interrupted class yesterday. It was probably her. I bet they

both plotted to take Miss Tremula's shoes
to get me into trouble. I'm going to go
and find Angelica after I've seen
Madame Dupré."

"Do you think that's a good idea?"
Bella asked anxiously.

Peri agreed. "Remember it was
Angelica who cast that spell that made
you break your leg last year. She might
do it again! Why don't you let us have a
word with her instead?"

"No," Nina said defiantly. "I'm not
going to let the Nightshade family beat
me. Anyway, Angelica wouldn't dare
hurt me again – not after she got caught
out last time!"

Nina solemnly fluttered off to Madame
Dupré's office.

She knows I'm not a thief, she
consoled herself.

Holly was in the office when Nina
arrived, fiddling with a tulip in her hair

and chattering away cheerfully to the
headmistress.

Nina sighed. It doesn't look like *she's*
been told off, she thought.

Madame Dupré noticed Nina in the
doorway. "Come in and sit down,
Nina." She pointed to one of
the toadstools by her desk.
"Miss Marram has told
me all about last
night's little
adventure. I
must say that
I am very
disappointed in
you, Nina. You
have upset your
teacher, who thinks the
world of you, and Miss
Marram also tells me that
you must have used magic
to get the shoes. There was
evidence of some very

strong dark fairy magic when we retraced your flight from Miss Tremula's studio."

Nina shook her head. "I'm sorry, Madame, but Miss Marram is mistaken. I've got nothing to do with the shoes going missing. I've no idea how Holly got them. She came into the studio to say she'd lost her bag."

"Yes," said the headmistress, "and she found it with *your* bag. Why did you take Holly's bag, Nina? As if taking Miss Tremula's shoes wasn't bad enough. I have been told how fascinated you had been by them earlier in the day. In any case, unfortunately theft is not the only thing I have to talk to you about. Holly tells me that you have not been looking after her properly. And Miss Marram has backed this up. Apparently she had to find her own way to class *and* you crashed into her in the corridor—"

"But, Madame," Nina protested, "it

was an accident! And I did try to take her to class, but she flew away from me."

"Nina, do not interrupt me," the headmistress scolded. "I know that some First Years can be a little difficult. It is only natural, as it is their first time away from home, but I chose you to be a mentor because I thought you would set a good example to Holly. It seems I was wrong."

"Please, Madame!" Nina was crying now. "It's not fair — I've been doing my best, you have to believe me."

"All this is most unlike you, it's true," the headmistress agreed kindly. "But you must understand that if I have any more reports of this kind of behaviour, I will have to talk to your mother. Now dry your eyes and take Holly to class. And then you must go and apologize to Miss Tremula. She is still very upset."

Nina shot Holly a look of anger and muttered: "Come on then, slow-wings. We don't want you getting 'lost' again, do we?"

Holly grinned mischievously, but the smile faded fast when she saw who was waiting for her in the corridor.

"Angelica!" she gasped.

"Polly!" Angelica countered. The older fairy was hovering by Madame Dupré's door, a smaller fairy fluttering behind her. Peri and Bella were there too.

"But you said your name was Holly," said Nina, puzzled.

"*This* is Holly," said Angelica,

gesturing to a small fairy with a rose in
her blonde hair.

"TWINS!" Nina cried.

Chapter Ten

Angelica was furious that her twin sisters had played such a dirty trick. "It's lucky for you, Nina, that you have such good friends," she said. "I warned you, Holly, didn't I? Do you want to end up scrubbing the floors as a punishment?"

"You could be the char-fairy of Charlock!" Peri joked.

"Don't wind them up," Bella hissed. "Angelica *has* helped us out this time."

"S'pose so," Peri said reluctantly. "Anyway, you were wrong about

Angelica, Nina. Her twin sisters carried
out their little plan all on their own."

"We confronted Angelica
about the missing pointe
shoes," Bella explained,
"and we told her
about Holly
appearing and
disappearing all over
the place. We thought
they had both been using
magic, you see."

"But it was
nothing to do
with me, so I
realized right
away that Polly must
have been involved," said
Angelica angrily. "They do
this kind of thing all the time
at home. It drives me potty. I
thought I'd got rid of them
when I came here, but then

Mum went and put Holly's name down
for the Academy too."

"And I thought Poppy was an
annoying little sister!" Nina cried. "But
that doesn't explain why Polly's here,"
she added. "Does Madame know about
Polly?"

"Actually," said Polly, "it's
Polyanthus, but that's too tricky for most
common—"

"Yeah, I know," Nina interrupted
irritably.

"What is going on?" asked a stern
voice. Madame Dupré had entered the
corridor. "I think you had better come
back into my office, fairies. It looks like
you Nightshade fairies have been flying
rings around Nina for long enough."

Holly was made to explain how she and
Polly kept switching places so that it
appeared that Holly was popping up all
over the place. When Nina thought

Holly had lost her way, the little fairy had simply hidden and allowed her twin to go to class ahead of her.

"I knew there was something odd about the different flowers in your hair," said Nina.

"But you weren't clever enough to work it out, were you?" Holly retorted.

"Enough!" cried the headmistress. "And the shoes?" she asked. "How do you explain that?"

Holly looked at the floor and tried to hide a smirk. She was obviously very pleased that no one had managed to solve that little puzzle. "Polly used magic to take the shoes from Miss Tremula's studio during class, and I was waiting outside to hide them. Nina almost spotted me in the corridor, but I was too quick for her," she said, grinning. "I was going to put them back during the night, but I got stopped by Miss Marram," she said.

Polly looked rather bashful. "I'm

sorry, Nina. It was supposed to be a bit of fun. Holly heard you talking about the shoes before you crashed into her. We couldn't resist trying them. You made them sound so wonderful! And when Holly got caught, her story about *you* taking them seemed like a good idea."

"But you lied to Miss Marram," said Nina hotly. "You told her I had stolen them."

"I didn't think I was going to get caught, did I?" said Holly rudely.

"Your mother will come and collect you immediately, Polly," said Madame Dupré sternly. "You are not even supposed to be here. And we don't allow magic at the Academy – it is our Number One Rule. However, as you are not officially a pupil here, Polly, there is nothing I can do about it."

Polly gulped. "I know, Madame. I'm sorry."

"How come your mum hasn't twigged

you're missing?" Bella asked.

Polly sighed. "I'm supposed to be at drama school," she explained. "Mum packed me off to the Shakespindle Stage School, but I really didn't want to go there, so I faked Mum's writing and sent them a letter saying I was coming here instead. Holly and I have never been separated before."

"That's why Mum made you go to different schools!" Angelica cried. "You're always in trouble when you're together!"

"The Shakespindle Stage School!" Peri butted in. "I would give my right wing to go there."

"I wish *you'd* both go there right now," Angelica shouted at her sisters.

"Actually, that's a great idea," Peri wittered on, oblivious to the argument going on around her. "Willow Shakespindle's written a fab play for twins. It's called *An Error in Comedy*. It'd be perfect for you two—"

"SILENCE!" cried Madame Dupré, waving her wand in exasperation. A haze of golden stars settled on the fairies, and Peri stopped twittering. "You are to go to the stage school as planned, Polly," she commanded, "and you, Holly, are under strict instructions to obey orders from now on. As for you, Nina, I hope you will accept my heartfelt apologies."

Nina curtseyed gratefully. Then she and her friends left the Nightshade sisters with Madame Dupré.

"That's that then," said Peri happily. "Let's hope Holly settles down now and

doesn't cause you any more hassle,
Nina."

"Yes," Nina agreed.

Bella started laughing. "Well, Nina,
we know you don't do things by halves,"
she said, "but who'd have thought you'd
land yourself with *double trouble*?"

Log on to

Nina
Fairy Ballerina
.com

for magical games, activities and fun!

Experience the magical world of Nina and her friends at the Royal Academy of Fairy Ballet. There are games to play, fun activities to make or do, plus you can learn more about the Nina Fairy Ballerina books!

Log on to www.ninafairyballerina.com now!

Collect three tokens and get this gorgeous Nina Fairy Ballerina ballet bag!

There's a token at the back of each Nina Fairy Ballerina book - collect three tokens, and you can get your very own, totally FREE Nina Fairy Ballerina ballet bag.

Send your three tokens, along with your name, address and parent/guardian's signature
(you must get your parent/guardian's permission to take part in this offer)
to: Nina Fairy Ballerina Ballet Bag Offer, Marketing Department, Macmillan Children's Books, 20 New Wharf Road, London N1 9RR

Nina Fairy Ballerina Bag Offer

1 Token

Collect 3 tokens and get your free ballet bag!
Valid until 31/12/06

A selected list of titles available from Macmillan Children's Books

ANNA WILSON

NINA FAIRY BALLERINA New Girl	ISBN-13: 978-0-330-43985-5 ISBN-10: 0-330-43985-5	£3.99
NINA FAIRY BALLERINA Daisy Shoes	ISBN-13: 978-0-330-43986-2 ISBN-10: 0-330-43986-3	£3.99
NINA FAIRY BALLERINA Best Friends	ISBN-13: 978-0-330-43987-9 ISBN-10: 0-330-43987-1	£3.99
NINA FAIRY BALLERINA Show Time	ISBN-13: 978-0-330-43988-6 ISBN-10: 0-330-43988-X	£3.99
NINA FAIRY BALLERINA Flying Colours	ISBN-13: 978-0-330-44622-8 ISBN-10: 0-330-44622-3	£3.99

All Pan Macmillan titles can be ordered from our website,
www.panmacmillan.com, or from your local bookshop
and are also available by post from:

Bookpost, PO Box 29, Douglas, Isle of Man IM99 1BQ
Credit cards accepted. For details:
Telephone: 01624 677237
Fax: 01624 670923
Email: bookshop@enterprise.net
www.bookpost.co.uk

Free postage and packing in the United Kingdom